FRIENDSHIP STORIES

Author, poet and translator, Deepa Agarwal writes for both children and adults and has over fifty books published. Among various other awards, she has received the N.C.E.R.T. National Award for Children's Literature in 1993 for her picture book *Ashok's New Friends*, while her historical fiction *Caravan to Tibet* was on the IBBY (International Board on Books for Young People) Honour List 2008.

Published by Scholastic India Pvt. Ltd.
A subsidiary of Scholastic Inc., New York, 10012 (USA).
Publishers since 1920, with international operations in Canada, Australia, New Zealand, the United Kingdom, India, and Hong Kong.

For information regarding permission, write to:
Scholastic India Pvt. Ltd.
A-27, Ground Floor, Sigma Centre
Infocity-1, Sector 34, Gurgaon-122001 (India)

ISBN-13: 978-93-5275-902-6

First edition: July 2019

This reprint edition: May 2024

Printed in India at MicroPrints India, New Delhi

FRIENDSHIP STORIES

Deepa Agarwal

SCHOLASTIC
New York Toronto London Auckland
Sydney New Delhi Hong Kong

A MESSAGE FROM SCHOLASTIC INDIA

Making friends, standing up to bullies, learning kindness and empathy, and drooling over mouth-watering food—these are just some of the ingredients of the stories in this book. These stories aren't only about friendship, they're stories of childhood and all that comes with it.

Deepa Agarwal's writing has always been contemporary and appealing to so many generations.

Hope you like it!

Shantanu Duttagupta
Publisher

For my grandchildren

Adya, Kartik, Aanya, Anika and Ahan

CONTENTS

A CATERPILLAR CALLED MATTHEW

The surroundings—rows of deodar trees spreading up the hill against an achingly blue sky—were beautiful. But the gravelled path didn't make for smooth progress. I was scrambling to catch up with Shweta's long strides when she suddenly stopped short. 'Hi Sky!' she called out.

Confused, I caught my breath and glanced at her questioningly. What was Shweta saying? It sounded like the nonsense rhymes we liked to sing when we were little kids—'Why?' 'Because the sky is so high!' etcetera, etcetera.

Then I realized that she was addressing the girl approaching us. A tall, plump girl with a mop of unruly curls and a round jolly face. Her black-rimmed spectacles had slid halfway down her nose.

'Hey Sky, meet Geeti Ahuja,' Shweta continued, her voice loud and hearty as ever. 'She's new.'

I was indeed brand new at boarding school and Shweta, whom I knew 'from home' had taken me under her wing. She was introducing me to all her friends, which I really appreciated. It was strange and lonesome being new, and I've always been a bad mixer. But I couldn't help feeling a little conscious too, that Shweta had to do it because her parents must have told her. That it must be a little boring for her, having me tag along. We were very different people—she was the chatty, sporty kind while I was quite the bookworm and didn't talk much.

'Hi ... uh, Sky,' I mumbled awkwardly. Surely that was not her real name, I couldn't help thinking. But what an odd nickname!

She must have read my thoughts because she replied with an impish grin, 'It's Akashvani Rai Chowdhary, actually.'

This sounded even stranger than Sky. 'Akashvani!' I burst out, forgetting my shyness, as well as forgetting that I was being rather rude. 'That's your name?'

'Yup! It is.' She grinned again.

'Wow!' I just couldn't stop myself. 'Who named you?'

'My grandfather,' she said. 'He was very fond of listening to the radio. All India Radio—Akashvani.' Her eyes twinkled so merrily behind her glasses that I couldn't help giggling. And somehow it felt okay. As if she knew that I wasn't laughing at her odd name, but enjoying it with her.

I couldn't help throwing a curious look at the cardboard box she was holding. It had a lot of holes punched into the lid.

'Hey Geeti, meet Matthew,' she chuckled, opening it up. It was full of leaves.

Matthew? I glanced around, puzzled. I couldn't see any Matthew-type person around and this was a strictly girls' school. But after Sky and Akashvani, anything seemed possible!

'Matthew is a caterpillar,' Shweta said, nudging me gently.

'A caterpillar!' My eyes almost popped out. Then I saw him—the fuzzy green caterpillar in the box, almost lost in his nest of broad dock leaves.

'Say "Hi" to Matthew, Geeti,' Sky said.

I gaped at her, but she was absolutely serious.

'Hi Matthew,' I said softly, feeling quite silly. But it seemed to me the creature actually stopped munching to look up!

'He likes you,' Sky chortled, closing the box.

'Does he?' I was idiotically pleased. The truth was, I'd been feeling rather low. Coming to a boarding school in the middle of the term was an upsetting experience, even though this was something that had been discussed at home for a long time. Both my parents had jobs that compelled them to keep long hours and I happened to be an only child. My dadi was there to supervise the help, but she didn't keep very good health. Then Mamma got selected for some training abroad and that settled it. Before I knew it, my bags were packed for boarding school.

Naturally, at that moment I was feeling rather marooned.

Of course, it was idiotic. Feeling thrilled that a caterpillar liked me. He could not possibly. At eleven, I was old enough to know better—caterpillars didn't have feelings. But I sensed that in a roundabout way Sky was saying that she liked me. This thought warmed me like a blast of sunshine on a January morning. At that moment, I badly needed a friend.

It was the games period and girls were racing around in the playing fields in front of us. 'Excuse me,' Shweta said. 'I have to go for basketball practice.' She jogged off gracefully.

That left Sky and me. 'Are you good at games?' she asked. 'I'm awful,' she continued, without waiting for an answer. 'Come, let's collect some leaves for Matthew. He is a real glutton.'

Below the oak trees that bordered the playground there was a gradual slope. It was thickly overgrown with dock leaves, ferns, sour grass and all sorts of wild plants. I followed Sky with careful steps, a little nervous that I might tumble over. Negotiating a hillside was another new experience for me. Cautiously, I began to pluck the long, broad dock leaves that Sky said were Matthew's favourite food, trying not to think of the creepy crawlies that might be lurking in the foliage. But I didn't want to look like a darpok.

'Hey, what's this? Wow!' Sky exclaimed, quite excited. 'Look Geeti, look what I found—a porcupine quill!'

'A porcupine quill?' Awed, I took it from her and gazed at it. A long spike, off-white with blackish-brownish stripes in between. How strange it was—like an extraordinarily long, thin and pointed finger nail. 'Wow! You mean to say porcupines actually come here?'

Being so new and all, I couldn't help feeling a little suspicious that she might be pulling my leg.

'Of course. There are all kinds of animals around here. Rabbits, foxes and jackals too. And ...' her voice went down to a whisper, 'panthers. But usually in winter, when there's hardly anyone around,' she ended, laughing. She had seen the terrified look in my eyes. Her laugh was plump and solid, just like her. It made you feel like laughing too. I began to hand the quill back. But she waved me away and said, 'Keep it. It's for you.'

'Oh no,' I said awkwardly. 'You found it. You keep it.'

'So what? I'm giving it to you. Keep it, Geeti. It's supposed to be lucky.' She patted my back so emphatically that I felt I had no choice but to accept it.

'Really lucky?' I asked. She nodded vigorously.

I had never heard that porcupine quills were supposed to be lucky. For all I knew, she had made it up on the spot. But I had never come across one before. And it felt just too wonderful to get a good luck charm on my very first day in a new school. Later, I put it away carefully in my locker.

Already, it didn't feel that bad being banished to boarding school.

Still, it took me some time to get over my homesickness altogether.

It was my third night in school. The huge dormitory with its rows of beds felt cold and empty, in spite of all the girls sleeping around me. I missed my cosy little room, especially the fact that if I needed anything, Mamma and Dad were just across the passage. Here, when scary shadows waved at the windows and the wooden floor creaked spookily, all I could do was cower under my quilt and try to quieten my frantically beating heart. I was actually crying that night when I heard a whisper, 'Geeti!' For a moment, my heart stopped with fright.

Then, 'It's me—Sky,' reassured me. 'Listen,' she whispered, 'I got a parcel from home. Come and try some of the goodies.'

I slipped out of bed and followed her, quiet as a mouse. It didn't strike me to ask why the goodies were to be consumed in the hidey-hole under the stairs at midnight, rather than in the dining room at teatime as usual. But deliciously crumbly besan laddus and mathri with achar had never tasted better than they did that night. And when I crept back to bed, I fell asleep the moment my head hit the pillow!

Soon I fell into the routine. I got used to boarding school life and Sky became my closest friend. But what an odd girl she was! And how she adored Matthew! She had long conversations with him. One-sided ones, of course. How could one get so attached to a caterpillar, I couldn't help wondering? But then, I realized it was the only kind of pet one could keep in boarding school.

'Why did you call him Matthew?' I asked one day. I too had kept caterpillars, but had never thought of naming them.

'We-ell,' she said thoughtfully, 'Matthew–it's a stately sort of a name. And he looks stately, doesn't he?'

I looked down at Matthew, moving slowly and sluggishly among the leaves. Munching away without a care in the world. Yes, he was stately. Matthew suited him perfectly as a name.

'Imagine,' I said, 'soon he'll turn into a butterfly and fly away ...'

'Oh-n-no, please don't remind me.' Sky looked almost tearful.

It was a real shock—to see her looking sad. I was so used to her giggling all the time.

'I can't bear the thought,' she continued, 'Matthew flying away. It's too awful.'

I stared at her. What a funny girl, I thought. Why had she kept a caterpillar as a pet? Everyone knows that caterpillars have to turn into butterflies someday. And it looked to me that Matthew was going to become one any day now. He would soon turn into a chrysalis and then into a butterfly. Which could never be kept in a box if you wanted it to live ...

But Sky did not want to face that fact. It made me feel terrible for her, that she would have to lose Matthew. But what could anyone do?

The next morning, it happened. Sky had been sent to the dormitory after breakfast to sew on a button missing on her blouse. I ran to feed Matthew.

But when I opened the box, he wasn't there! Only a lifeless-looking chrysalis ...

I felt like crying. Poor Sky! What would she do without Matthew? It was too awful for words.

Suddenly, I remembered something. While collecting leaves, I'd seen another caterpillar. The spitting image of Matthew! His twin, I'd thought with a smile. Suppose ... I dashed out at once? There was no time to lose. Luckily, I found the caterpillar. Carefully, I carried it back on a leaf. I had just lowered it into the box when Sky walked into the room.

'Have you fed Matthew?' she asked anxiously.

'Yeah, yeah!' I was quite breathless.

She took the box from me. 'Hi, old Fuzzy-Wuzzy,' she said affectionately. I held my breath. But it was all right. She hadn't caught on!

After that, I kept an eye out for caterpillars of the Matthew breed. Fortunately, there were plenty around. As soon as the latest 'Matthew' showed signs of being ready for a change over, I quietly popped in the next one.

I was on to my third Matthew, when Sky suddenly asked me one day, 'Do you think there's something wrong with Matthew?' She looked quite worried.

'What do you mean?' I asked, feeling uneasy, but trying not to show it.

'Well, he's taking a rather long time to turn into a butterfly. Do ... do you think he's suffering from some kind of deficiency?' she frowned.

'Uh ... well-I-I don't think so,' I stammered. I pretended to examine Matthew closely. 'He looks perfectly fine to me. No need for tonics! Ha, ha!' I tried to laugh at my own feeble joke. 'And m-maybe some caterpillars take longer than others.'

Sky gave me a funny look. Maybe I stuttered too much. 'Another odd thing,' she said slowly. 'He seems to keep changing in size—grows smaller and bigger, bigger and smaller ...'

Bigger and smaller! My face went red. Naturally, each time, I'd chosen a slightly smaller caterpillar, so he'd last longer. I couldn't choose another Matthew that was just about to change, could I?

'What nonsense!' I began. 'You must be imagining ...'

Then I stopped short. Sky's gaze was fixed on me, meaningfully. Her eyes were twinkling.

My heart lurched. She knows, I thought!

'You knew!' I cried out. 'You knew all along!' I felt like a complete idiot.

'Obviously,' she replied, smiling. 'Caterpillars don't generally shrink.'

'Then why ...' I began indignantly, and gave up. Because she was laughing her fat, rollicking laugh which made me laugh too, it was so infectious. We laughed and laughed till we were breathless and our stomachs ached.

'You nut,' she said finally. 'You crazy, silly nut! You kept changing caterpillars on me and I didn't have the heart to tell you I'd guessed.' She squeezed my arm and her eyes misted behind her glasses. 'You didn't have to do that. It was just a caterpillar.'

'No,' I said firmly. 'Not just a caterpillar. He was a caterpillar called Matthew!'

THE BEST HANUMAN

Anita clasped the shiny string of beads round her neck and examined herself in the mirror. The reflection wasn't too clear because the mirror, which hung on the soot-grimed wall of their one-room tenement, was old and tarnished. All the same, what she saw satisfied her. Her new (well, almost!) yellow satin kurta worn over a matching salwar brightened up her peaky little face. So did the gold and red bindi she had borrowed from her mother. Amma had grumbled a bit, saying that at twelve she was too young to dress up so much, but had finally agreed.

Flinging a spangled chunni round her neck she ran and peeped out of the window. The brilliant October sunshine was slowly dissolving into a shadowy dusk and the narrow lane seemed noisier than usual. Vendors pushing handcarts laden with vegetables and fruit competed with those hawking shimmering glass bangles, toy bows and arrows and Hanuman and Ravana masks; all yelling to draw attention to their wares. The festival of Dussehra, which commemorated Lord Rama's victory over the ten-headed demon Ravana, was just a few days away and the excitement seemed to infect everyone.

'He'll be here any minute,' her mother's voice came from behind her. Amma was kneading dough for their evening chapattis in a big brass platter, even though Anita had said that she'd like to eat at the Ramlila she was planning to attend.

It was the Ramlila that made Dussehra so special for her. The enactment of the story of Rama's adventures went on for ten days and kept Anita enthralled. Rama was so good, so brave, his wife Sita so gentle and pretty, Lakshmana such a devoted brother. Rama's exile to the forest brought tears to her eyes as did Sita's abduction by the wicked Ravana. Rama's loyal follower, the monkey-god Hanuman, performed feats of strength which quite took her breath away, while the capers of his monkey army made her laugh till her stomach ached. And when Rama finally defeated the monstrous Ravana, she cheered as loudly as she could.

On these ten days, the daily drudgery passed by as pleasantly as a song from one of her favourite Hindi movies. Rushing home from school, quickly bolting down a cold chapatti and then dashing off again to help her mother with her afternoon round of cleaning and washing dishes in rich people's houses hardly seemed a grind as she waited for the evening to come.

And this evening was going to be special. Her older brother Mohan had said he'd return home early from work to take her to the big, fancy Ramlila which was far more elaborate than anything she had ever seen.

'Hundreds and thousands of rupees are spent on the sets alone,' Mohan had said. 'They say Hanuman ji actually flies!'

'How do they manage that?' Anita had asked, wide-eyed.

'They have ways,' Mohan had shrugged. Anita suspected he didn't know either but thought it better to keep quiet. If Mohan got irritated, he might just call off the plan or go by himself.

'Anita didi! Anita didi!' An all-too-familiar voice wiped the smile from her face. It was Veena, her young neighbour, who lived close by. Though she was barely seven years old, she was quite attached to Anita. Anita was fond of her too, but sometimes she got fed up of babysitting Veena—especially when her mother dumped her at their place while she was busy with something else.

Had Veena got wind of their plans? If she saw Anita all dressed up, she'd insist on tagging along. How would they look after her? Veena was hard to control. She might even get lost in the crowd.

'Aren't you going to open the door?' her mother scolded as Veena rattled the door chain loudly.

Anita's thin face bunched into a mask of irritation as she stomped to the door.

'Oh—h! Just look at you!' Veena gasped. 'All dressed up? When did you get this salwar suit? I know—you're going to the big Ramlila!' And sure enough, just as Anita had been dreading, she whined, 'I want to come too! Can't I, Mausi?'

Amma smiled. She doted on Veena—actually few people could resist that pest, all because of her pert features, big eyes and curly mop. 'Of course, child. But you must go and ask your mother first.'

The moment Veena left, Anita exploded. 'Amma! Why did you have to agree? How will we take care of her?'

'She's not a babe in arms,' her mother replied, frowning. She continued in a gentler tone. 'You know how much her father helps us. It was he who got Mohan that job in the grocery store and loaned us money for the rent when we were short last month. It's a small thing to do in return.'

Anita's face went still. She knew very well how dependent they were on Veena's father, Shivdas Chacha. He had stood by them, ever since her father had died in a road accident. Well, she thought sighing, the pest would have to be tolerated as best they could.

But why was Mohan taking so long? Amma was lighting the kerosene stove, preparing to roll out the chapattis. Normally, Anita helped her but she didn't want to get flour all over her nice clothes. She went and sat outside near the door so she could spot Mohan the moment he turned the corner. The delicious aroma of onions being browned with spices came to her, making her stomach rumble—one of the neighbours cooking dinner, perhaps. Then the heady scent of jasmine filled the air. Nagamma, who lived next door, stepped out, carrying a basket full of the little flower garlands women liked to wear in their hair. She sold them at the traffic lights. Suddenly Anita longed to buy one to decorate her skinny plait.

She had four ten-rupee notes rolled up in a handkerchief—money Amma had allowed her to keep when she was paid last month. She had planned to spend it at the Ramlila, on chole, aloo tikki or whatever other mouthwatering goodies were on offer there.

Of course, Mohan would have enough cash for their bus fare and the snacks. But Anita wanted to spend hers too. The thought of having her own money to do as she wished was so exhilarating! It wiped out that horrid feeling of always being needy and helpless.

Another idea, a rather crazy one, had been buzzing in her mind. She could donate the money for a token award to the best actor, the way she had seen people do at the smaller Ramlila organized near their house. She imagined them announcing it. 'For the actor playing the part of Hanuman ji, Anita Rani is pleased to announce a prize of forty rupees.' Her face flushed at the thought. People would wonder who the generous lady was and the applause that followed would be as much for her as for the actor. Yes, she wasn't too hard up to express her appreciation for something she had enjoyed. So, she resisted the temptation and held on to the notes.

A boy carrying a stand of toy bows and arrows, red, wrapped with silver tinsel, and swords made of foil and cardboard came into view. When they were little, Mohan would always buy a set. She was smiling at the memory when Veena came tearing down the road, her frilly dress flouncing around her. Her eyes were dark with kajal and pink bows, matching her frock, jogged up and down on her head.

'Hasn't Mohan bhaiya come as yet?' she squealed. 'We'll be late. Ooh, I want to buy a sword!'

'What'll you do with it?' Anita frowned.

'Play Ramlila till Mohan bhaiya comes!'

Anita suppressed an exasperated sigh. 'Don't be silly, girls don't play with swords,' she said.

'Of course they do! What about the Queen of Jhansi?' Veena pouted. 'You told me how brave she was and how she fought the British army. Don't you want me to be brave?' Then her large eyes narrowed, 'Oh, sorry, I forgot. You couldn't be having any money. I'll go home and—'

'No!' Anita's voice deafened her own ears. 'I've got some.' Her throat felt funny and swollen as she took out the much folded notes and beckoned to the vendor. She tried not to think about the grandiose plans she had made for this money and concentrated on haggling with the hawker, managing to save half of it.

Veena began to flourish her sword, imitating the fencing bouts she had seen in the movies and almost missed hitting a woman passing by in the crowded street.

'Sit down,' Anita cried. 'I'll tell you the story of today's episode. It's very sad—Lord Rama is going to be banished to the forest because his stepmother, Kaikeyi, wants her son to be king.'

'I want to hear Hanuman's story,' Veena insisted. 'How he flew over the seas and brought back a whole mountain to get sanjivani, the miraculous herb, to save Lakshmana's life. Oh, look—there's a man selling Hanuman masks. I want one! I want one!'

'Girls—' Anita began.

'Girls can play at being anything,' Veena said quickly. 'And I like Hanuman ji best in the Ramlila.'

And I want to give you a good spanking, Anita thought. She pulled out the two ten-rupee notes she had left. Thankfully, the man agreed to sell the plastic mask for that amount. Anita slipped the elastic band over Veena's curls and said, 'Okay, sit down and I'll tell you the story.' Inwardly she was cursing Mohan for taking so long. She would have saved her money if he'd come on time.

She began mechanically noticing that one by one the lights were coming on in the houses down the street. Disappointment tugged at the corners of her mouth as she continued with the tale. When would Mohan arrive? Suppose Amma said it was too late to go and they should postpone it for tomorrow? As it was she had agreed with great difficulty, saying that the neighbourhood Ramlila was good enough. But would Mohan's boss let him off early again?

'Girls! Come and eat,' Amma's voice interrupted her thoughts.

'No, Mausi, no,' Veena called, springing up. 'I'm not hungry. Come and watch my Ramlila. See, I'm Hanuman ji! I'm going to carry the whole mountain back so the doctor can look for the herb himself.'

Veena began to scamper about like a monkey. She picked up a piece of broken brick and hoisted it up, straining and panting as if it were a real mountain. Amma giggled like a girl, hiding her mouth with the end of her sari. Anita couldn't help smiling too, Veena's act was so comical. Several other laughs rang out and someone clapped and cried out, 'Jai Hanuman ji!'

With a start, Anita noticed that some passers-by had stopped and were watching Veena's antics with great amusement. A frown crumpled her brow when she noticed that the mask vendor was among them too.

'Stop it!' she hissed, suddenly self-conscious.

But Veena was enjoying all the attention. Her shrill voice drowned Anita's out as she proclaimed, 'Anita didi, that Ravana mask will be just right for you,' pointing to a replica of the ten-headed demon that was among the vendor's wares. 'If you put it on, we can play at a proper Ramlila.'

There was a huge outburst of laughter. 'A proper Ramlila!' a short, stout man guffawed. 'But this Ravana is too small and puny, he'll be knocked down before the battle begins!'

Suddenly a wave of fury swept over Anita. Why did she have to put up with all this? Would nothing go right today?

'I act Ravana? You horrid girl!' she burst out, angry tears pouring down her cheeks. 'I spent all my money buying you a sword and a mask, I'm taking you to the Ramlila too and still you insist on making fun of me!'

'Arre, arre, what's all this?'

In the faint half-light, Anita glimpsed a tall, lean figure with a familiar gait coming down the street, white teeth gleaming in a dark face.

'Mohan bhaiya, Mohan bhaiya!' both girls called out together.

'It's just a game, isn't it?' Mohan said, patting Anita's flaming cheek. 'And this Ramlila seems even more entertaining than the big one! We won't have such a pretty Ravana there, nor a Hanuman for that matter,' he grinned.

Anita wiped her eyes with the corner of her chunni, carefully. Could she go and powder her nose again or would Mohan tease her?

'Are we ready to leave or do I have a minute to make myself pretty too?' he went on. Unable to speak, she nodded vigorously. And then a small hand clutched hers.

'Anita didi, Anita didi, don't cry.' Something papery scratched her palm. 'That short man gave it to me,' Veena whispered. 'He said I was the best Hanuman he'd ever seen and he should know, since he'd played the role many times. And—and, he gave me these passes. He said they're for the big Ramlila and we deserved really good seats. I-I even asked for an extra one for Mohan bhaiya!'

Anita stared at the crumpled note—ten—no fifty rupees! She pushed it back into Veena's hand but the little girl wailed, 'You're still angry with me. I didn't mean to upset you—I thought you'd have fun playing Ravana!'

Anita sighed and hugged Veena. 'It's okay,' she whispered. 'I'm sorry for acting so silly.'

The big Ramlila was even grander than Anita had imagined. And when Anita Rani announced her award for the actor who played Sita, the applause was deafening. She had to agree, though, that Veena was not that much of a pest. After all, she was the best Hanuman ever!

Just Balloons

The party was halfway over. Ten-year-old Tara sighed with relief, though she knew the worst was yet to come. She hated birthday parties. She hated the noise, the screaming, especially the way they ended—with everyone pulling all the balloons off the walls and bursting them. Ever since she was a really tiny kid, she had loved balloons. There was something so bouncy and happy about them. Sometimes she felt she could actually fly off to some wonderful place, holding onto a balloon. She knew they would deflate eventually, but why burst them?

Someone pushed her aside roughly. Tara winced, trying to regain her balance.

'Sorry, DD!' It was Medha, and the grin on her broad face showed that she wasn't sorry at all.

Tara turned red. She hated being called 'DD'—'delicate darling'. But that was what everyone called her. Medha had started it. And when Medha started something, everyone had to follow.

More kids brushed past. The cake was about to be cut. Tara edged to the back of the crowd.

'Hey,' someone said, 'don't you want to see the cake getting cut?' The boy looked vaguely familiar, though Tara wasn't sure where she had seen him. His brown eyes were glittering, his cheeks flushed. He was as excited as everyone else.

There was no time to reply because a loud cheer went up, followed by hearty claps. Ananya, the birthday girl, had blown out the candles and was cutting the cake. Her mother popped a piece into her mouth. Someone started slicing it to pass around. Medha grabbed a handful. She began to smear it on Ananya's face—more laughs.

BANG! Someone burst a balloon, right in Tara's ear. She jumped, turned around. It was the same boy. And even as Tara stared at him aghast, he burst the other two he was holding—red ones.

Everyone laughed loudly. 'What did you do, Abhay!' someone said. 'Poor DD. She's just too, too delicate!'

Tara couldn't bear it any longer. She dashed to the door and ran home.

'Party over already?' Ma asked.

Tara nodded.

'I suppose you didn't eat anything again?'

Tara knew what was coming. But somehow, she just couldn't lie to her mother. She nodded again.

Ma sighed. 'You must try to mix with the others, beta. How will you ever make any friends?'

Tara's face burned. It was not that she didn't want to make friends. But who wanted to be friends with someone known as DD? The butt of each and every joke?

The next morning when she got on the school bus, she got an unpleasant surprise. Abhay was there too. How hadn't she noticed him so far? School had reopened just few days ago. He was obviously new. But already he seemed on the best terms with everyone. Tara felt a pang of envy shoot through her. Apprehension too. Another tormentor added to the lot.

She shrank further into her corner seat. But it didn't help.

Because Medha, who entered just then, said, 'Hey, why did you run away from the party, DD?'

'Come on, Medha!' It was a boy named Sumit. 'Don't you know our dear little DD? She can't stand the company of ruffians like us!'

And everyone began to chant:

'Delicate Darling, Mamma's pet!
Is upset, is upset!
Very soon, she'll cry, I bet!
Tch-tch-tch, tch-tch-tch!'

Tara felt as if her face was on fire. She clenched her teeth, trying to stop the shameful tears from spilling out. Tried to glare back. But it was of no use.

The sight of those grinning, mocking faces was too much. The moment her eyes overflowed, however, she was surprised to see one person who wasn't laughing. Abhay—he looked—well—embarrassed?

Thankfully, the rest of the day was uneventful. In the afternoon, around four o'clock, her mother said, 'Tara, can you check the mailbox?'

Tara walked out, squinting in the hot sun. Then stopped short. What *was* that? Three red balloons, fluttering above the gate! Mystified, she inched closer. Who could have tied them there? And why? Was there a bomb inside one? Had someone marked their house for some reason? It took all the courage she could muster to tear the bunch off the gate. For a few minutes she stared stupidly at them. Should she just let them go, fly away and vanish?

But something stopped her. She hurried inside and crept into her room. Then sat on her bed for a while, holding the balloons, watching them bounce and bob in the breeze from the fan. There was nothing threatening about them now. She tied them to a nail in the wall and sat down to do her homework. However, she couldn't help sneaking a look at them now and again. Who'd left them there? Was it a prank? So far it hadn't harmed her, though.

Whatever it was, there was something cheery about those balloons. They felt almost like a gift, or a message. As if in some crazy way, someone felt she was worth reaching out to.

The next morning found her slumped in her corner in the bus again, as usual. And as usual, Medha clomped up the steps with a nasty grin on her face. 'Hi, DD!'

Tara's face puckered, Medha's grin grew broader. Tara's heart was sinking, sinking, right to the bottom when unexpectedly it bounced up again. The three red balloons, fluttering so carefree, flashed through her mind! To her utter astonishment, she found herself replying, 'Hi, BB!' Where did those words come from?

Medha's face darkened. 'BB! What do you mean?' Her voice was loud and threatening.

A sudden hush fell over the bus.

'BB!' Tara's voice was as clear as a bell. 'It means Big Bully!'

'Big Bully? How dare you!' Medha growled.

'But you are!' someone said softly. It was Abhay.

'Yes ... you are ...' someone else muttered. Then someone else, and someone else.

A thought exploded in Tara's mind. Three red balloons ... could it have been Abhay? But why?

A chorus of shouts drowned out her thoughts. 'BB!' 'BB!'

It grew so loud that Tara's heart leapt in horror. What had she begun? The look on Medha's face—shocked, terrified, didn't make it better.

'Stop! Please ... I didn't mean ...' she said. But no one listened. Luckily, a teacher stepped into the bus just then, and the clamour died down.

School arrived. Tara got off in a daze and began to walk to class. Then she heard someone call out, 'Tara!'

It was Abhay. 'Don't feel so bad,' he said. 'She needed a dose of her own medicine.' He paused, then continued. 'I'm really sorry, I didn't mean to upset you at the party that day.'

'It's okay!' Tara smiled. 'I really shouldn't be such a DD. But ... something happened yesterday. Someone—'

'Tied three red balloons to your gate?' he laughed. 'I wanted to say sorry, but didn't know how.'

'They worked like magic,' Tara said in a rush. 'I don't know how. For the first time, I could stand up to Medha.'

'Wow! But you know ... you're not as much of a DD as you think.'

'Thanks for helping me find that out. But I don't mind. As long as I'm not a BB.'

'That you'll never be!' Abhay laughed.

Tara was thankful for that. Thankful too, that at last she had found a friend!

MY LIFE IN PICTURES

The moment Vandita entered my room I knew it had not been a good idea to invite her home. Because her eyes zoomed straight onto the collage behind my bed. The collage that was actually my life in pictures. And I wasn't particularly keen to reveal my whole life to her.

I wanted to impress Vandita—whom we all secretly thought of as the queen of the classroom. This was something that had always puzzled me, because there was no particular reason why she should be the most admired girl in VII-B. She was neither good at studies or games, in dramatics or debate. She was not even a great dancer and could barely carry a tune. And yet whenever anyone mentioned Vandita, it was in a tone of hushed awe. Girls would cluster around her with silly grins on their faces the moment she appeared and say 'Hi, Vandita!' as if they were greeting a celebrity. She would respond with a faint Mona Lisa smile, without stopping to talk to anyone, and would make her way to her desk with an odd, rather grown-up expression as if we were too childish or rowdy for her. Instead of turning us off, it baffled us and made us all the more eager to be friends with her. But this proved easier said than done.

Because while Vandita was nice enough, she wouldn't let anyone get too close to her.

Till the day she asked me for help with her maths.

I was so completely bowled over that for a minute I couldn't say anything at all.

Finally, I was able to stammer, 'Y-yes, of course! P-please come over tomorrow afternoon.'

'Thanks so much,' she had said in her soft voice, sounding as formal as ever.

And now here she was in person, right inside my room—gazing at the collage that was the embarrassment of my life!

'Who made this?' she asked.

I stared at her. Her face was flushed, her brown eyes gleamed. I'd never seen her so excited. I squinted hard at her to try and guess if she were making fun of it.

'My mom,' I replied, sagging with silent despair. Yeah, my trigger-happy mom who thinks it's a matter of life and death to record each and every moment of our existence.

I cringed as Vandita's large eyes ran over the pictures—me as a ridiculously obese baby, perched inside a bathtub—completely naked. Me, waving a spoon with disgusting gobs of food smeared all over my face. Me, with my mouth wide open, howling like a lunatic. Me, as a toddler with my dress lifted up to my waist, displaying my panties without a care in the world. And then I had to suppress a scream—me on the potty! How could Mom have done that? Was it that important to record my very first civilized pee? Why hadn't it ever occurred to me to tear off that horrendous photo? Oh, why did I agree to help Vandita with her maths? And why did she ask me? From feeling like the most privileged girl in class, I had sunk to being the most shamefaced.

The truth was, this collage was one of the reasons I avoided asking anyone home, other than my closest friends Bhavya and Riddha. Even though they rarely spared the opportunity to scream with laughter whenever they happened to look up at it. I could take it from them—after all we had all grown up together and if they laughed too much, I could shut them up by reminding them of the million embarrassing moments in their lives I had witnessed. But Vandita!

Oh my God, now she had her eyes fixed on that awful picture—the one of the folk dance for the school annual function! The gaudy Haryanvi outfit, rings of kajal around my eyes making me look like an owl, one hip stuck out and an arm raised in a stupidly coy pose. Gawd, this was one moment I would have given anything to own a cloak of invisibility.

'Uh ... would you like a juice or something?' Had she noticed that my voice was almost tearful? 'Th-then we can get down to the-the problems ...'

'Oh, thanks, that would be great,' she replied in that soft, tinkling voice that reminded me of the sound of a dancer's ghungroos. Only, the ghungroos seemed to be much louder than I'd ever heard them.

I hurried to the kitchen and opened the fridge. I hadn't told my mother that a friend was coming over. I was too terrified that she might burst into the room to click the two of us engrossed in our studies—probably with the most ghastly expressions on our faces. Even though she'd made a pact with me—not to click any photographs except on special occasions like birthdays and festivals, and these too had to be approved before being printed and made into collages or preserved in albums for people to snigger over. In exchange, I had agreed to let the collage remain on my bedroom wall.

'Can't you understand, sweetie,' Mom had said, 'how important all these moments are for me? When I look at them, I think of you as an adorable little baby ...'

'Then why don't you keep them in your room?' I yelled.

Dad had cleared his throat. 'No room,' he said, rolling his eyes.

'And then, Purva,' Mom had continued in an almost tearful voice, 'whenever I enter your room, all those memories come flooding back.'

'Mom ... don't you like me the way I am now?' I had glared at her. Then, 'All right, all right!' when I saw the dangerous look on her face.

All the same, I was not too sure if my mother would keep her side of the bargain. She was too, too addicted to her camera. So, I was always careful. But as they say—man proposes and God disposes. So while I proposed to carry two glasses of apple juice neatly arranged on a tray along with a bowl of chips and a few generous slices of my mom's chocolate cake to my room, without anyone knowing, God was making other plans. Now about my mom's chocolate cake—it is something that almost makes up for her camera addiction. The yummiest thing that ever went into your mouth. Sometimes, I have a sneaky feeling that Bhavya and Riddha have remained my dearest friends since kindergarten because of this wonderful cake.

Luckily, Mom had baked just the day before and if there was something that could cancel out the embarrassing impression those crazy photos must have made, it was the cake. I was smiling to myself as I entered my room, congratulating myself on this particular stroke of luck, when what did I hear but my mom's voice at its highest, most enthusiastic pitch.

'Isn't that absolutely adorable? She was such a good baby. Unlike her brother, she took to the potty right away. Never ever did her business on the floor. We didn't believe in disposable diapers. At least I didn't. So bad for the environment!'

I almost dropped the tray. I wanted to scream and pull my hair. But I controlled myself somehow, reminded myself that I was almost twelve—quite grown-up. Next year, I would be a teenager. I should try and act mature, even though my mother couldn't.

Then Mom saw me. 'Purva,' she said, 'you never told me a friend was coming over.'

'I forgot, Mom,' I mumbled. Then I saw the camera in her hand. I put down the tray and took a deep breath. I looked sternly at my mother and shook my head. She looked down at the camera and bit her lip. I could guess at the struggle going on inside her. She looked pleadingly at me, but I shook my head again, even though somewhere I was feeling guilty about it. Mom's mouth drooped, her shoulders sagged and she nodded, then shrugged.

'Well, have fun, you two!' she said.

I sighed with relief. She was turning away when Vandita spoke in her tinkling, bell-like voice. 'Oh, Aunty, please ... could you take a picture of us together?'

My mouth fell open. Mom looked at me confused. Vandita flung us a puzzled look. I clenched my teeth and said, 'Yeah, Mom, why don't you?'

'All right,' she said expressionlessly.

She took several pictures, of course, in several poses. Vandita and me seated at my desk, frowning over mathematical problems. Vandita and me laughing at an imaginary joke, with our arms linked together, looking as if we were lifelong friends. And Vandita and I saying 'cheese' with all our might, just beneath the collage.

At that moment, I got a brainwave. Now I had a good excuse to tear up the collage. Mom had not kept her side of the bargain. I knew she'd make the excuse that it was Vandita who had asked but I would stand firm. After all, she could have said something like the camera battery was not charged or it just wasn't working or anything at all. She had exploited the situation and I would not forgive her for that.

Our study session went off okay. I went to see Vandita off at the gate and as she was leaving she said, 'Please, please e-mail all those photos to me. I'm dying to show them to my parents. Your mom is such a great photographer!'

'Of course,' I said. 'I'll ask her to transfer them to the computer right away. See you tomorrow in school!'

I would have to find a way to slip this in while having a showdown with Mom. In the meantime, I ran back to my room. My hands had been itching to tear up that horrible collage for so long that I could hardly wait.

But I found the wall bare. The collage was gone! Mom had been smart enough to remove it before I went on the rampage. At first, I felt cheated—then relieved—then oddly ashamed. The wall looked so empty!

'Have you gone crazy?' I scolded myself, as I dragged my feet to my parents' bedroom. You hated that thing and now that it's gone you're missing it? But I had to tell Mom about sending the photos to Vandita.

She was lying down on the bed and half sat up when she heard me enter. Her face went red. 'Well ... she asked me to take the pictures ... okay ... I violated our agreement—so—I've removed it!' she said in a rush.

I felt even more ashamed. She looked so worried and guilty. I had forced my mother to make explanations to me. It felt awful. Of course, Vandita had asked her. How could she have refused? And why was I making such a fuss over something as silly as a few baby pictures?

'It's okay, Mom,' I said, hanging my head. 'You couldn't help it. But ... I would never have destroyed the collage. How could I? Isn't it my life in pictures? My whole life till now?'

Mom burst into laughter. She laughed and laughed and gave me the tightest hug ever. Then she said, 'Wait a second, I'll put it on automatic and click this moment.'

I groaned inwardly. But of course, I agreed–even though I could picture the caption ... Well, after all how could my mom change? And then it struck me–did I want her to change? After all, this is what made her unique!

There's a little more to tell after this. Vandita printed out the photos and brought them to class. And no marks for guessing who is the most admired girl in class now!

THE GIRL IN THE GARDEN

Richa sat on the stone bench in the garden, looking up at the house. She had really liked it, when they first came here two months ago.

After staying in a cramped flat in Delhi, it was heavenly to live in an airy bungalow with a sloping roof. To have a big room all to herself with a wide window which looked out onto miles and miles of greenery. And to have a garden in which she could run and play as much as she wanted. It was full of flowers she could pick too—bunches and bunches of them.

'We have four huge mango trees, seven guava trees and I don't know how many papaya and banana trees,' she had written to her best friend Kavya, who was eleven years old like herself. She'll think I'm bragging, she'd thought with a smile.

But Richa wasn't smiling today. Her small round mouth drooped and her wide smooth forehead was crumpled in a frown. Even her springy, wavy hair seemed to hang limp and lank.

The place was so green, so beautiful, especially today after the sudden quick shower that had sprinkled all the leaves with dewy drops. But, so lonely! There was no one to talk to or play with here. The houses in this area, which was a little away from the main town, were far and few. The new friends she'd made in school couldn't visit her because of the distance. How she missed Kavya!

Richa let out a long, mournful sigh. I wish we could go back to Delhi, she thought.

Suddenly, the leaves rustled in the tall bush behind her. 'Ooh!' she gasped as a shower of raindrops rained down on her. She blinked and licked a drop off her lip. But it wasn't raining any more! Of course, someone had shaken the raindrops off the bush behind her. But who? Bewildered, she turned around. Strange, there was no one to be seen. Then, she heard a giggle.

'Who's that?' she cried, jumping up.

Furiously she searched the bush, parted all the branches, shook them. She even went and looked behind it. But she couldn't find anyone. She didn't hear any footsteps either or catch a glimpse of someone running away. It was as if the trickster had vanished into thin air!

'Silly!' she said loudly. 'How childish and idiotic! Humph!'

Then she waited, holding her breath. The person might move, make a sound, give themselves away. But nothing happened. There was only a stillness, as if someone were holding their breath too—just like her. Then it came—peals and peals of tinkling laughter, as if that someone couldn't hold out any longer!

'Got you!' Richa cried, dashing towards the bush. She was convinced that the sound came from there. But her foot slipped on a slimy patch and she came down with a hard bump.

She heard more laughter now. Red-faced, wild, she got to her feet. 'Get lost!' she yelled out. 'Whoever you are! And don't you dare come here again.'

The laughter stopped at once. So suddenly that the silence rang in Richa's ears. And all at once she got the feeling that the person—whoever it was—had left. The air felt vacant and empty now, while before it had felt full ... somehow.

'What on earth have you been doing?' her mother cried out when she went in. Her jeans were all muddy, her face scratched. Mrs Malhotra was there as usual, having tea with her mother on the verandah. An older lady with her grey hair in a bun, she lived in the house next to theirs.

'Nothing,' Richa said sulkily. 'I just fell.'

'Go and change,' her mother said with a sigh. As she walked away, Richa heard her tell Mrs Malhotra,

'She has no company at all here. I wonder if we should take a house closer to town.'

Well, there was someone in the garden today, Richa thought, smiling now. It sounded like a girl. And she had to be living close by. Surely Mrs Malhotra would know? But hadn't she said there were no children in the neighbourhood?

I'll find out, Richa thought. I'll get that prankster!

The next afternoon, she deliberately went and sat on the stone bench again, though it was warm and sultry. She had the feeling that the girl would show up. And today she wouldn't let her get away.

She waited and waited, sweating, with the bees buzzing around her. She was about to get up and go when there was a rustle in the bushes and a shower of—well, flowers today! Sweet smelling *bela* flowers!

'Stop that!' she cried. 'Stop plucking our flowers and wasting them like that!'

'They're not your flowers,' was the reply. The voice sounded faint and distant for some reason. 'They're not from your garden.'

Richa didn't know what to say then. The voice was right. There were no bela bushes in their garden. Her mother had asked the mali to put one in, as a matter of fact. He'd seemed reluctant.

'They never survive in this garden,' he'd said. 'And I've been working here for a long time.'

'Well, try again,' her mother had said. Like Richa, she was not one to give up easily. So, she'd brought a plant herself and made him put it in. But it was not flowering as yet.

'All right,' Richa said finally. 'Will you stop acting silly and come out from wherever you're hiding?'

'And suppose I don't want to?' the voice said. It was slightly louder now.

'Why? Are you scared?' Richa shot back. There was something odd, something different about the way the girl spoke.

'What? Me scared?' Her voice was really loud now. She sounded indignant. 'I'll come out when I feel like and not because you're telling me to.'

'All right,' Richa sighed. 'Have it your own way. But you're a real bore—we could have such fun together.'

There was a long silence, as if she were thinking. Richa waited, biting her nails.

'All right,' she said finally. 'I'll come out. But close your eyes and open them only when I tell you to.'

You really are full of tricks, Richa thought. 'Okay,' she said aloud. And she closed her eyes tight and waited. This is stupid, she thought. I'm sure she's run off, leaving me sitting here like a fool. But the silence was so complete that it didn't seem possible anyone could be breathing, leave alone running.

'Open your eyes,' she heard.

Richa blinked. Then she saw the girl. She was tall, much taller than her. She had two long plaits and wore a rather odd-looking dress. It was silky, with puffy sleeves and reached way below her knees.

Is this why she wanted to hide? Richa thought, because she's dressed so funnily?

But the girl started giggling in such a delighted way that Richa felt she must be wrong. It must have been her love of mischief, because she really seemed like a prankster, if there ever was one.

'Are you a girl or a boy?' she asked Richa bluntly.

Richa was flabbergasted. 'Do I look like a boy?' she spluttered. 'Look at my hair.'

'Why are you wearing pants, then?' was the reply.

'Oh, come on, stop being silly. Surely you've seen girls in pants before!' Richa was bewildered, a little uneasy. Was she that backward?

The girl frowned, then shrugged. 'What's your name?' she asked, changing the topic.

'Richa. What's yours?'

'Bela,' replied the girl.

'Bela ...' Richa felt confused for a moment, as if something about the name should ring a bell. 'Do you stay close by?' she asked.

'Hmmm, yes.' The girl looked away. 'Come on,' she said. 'Let me show you something.'

She raced off down the gravel path right to the end of the garden, where there was an old, disused well. A little surprised, Richa followed. A cover had been put on top of it for safety. Richa had heard that someone had fallen into it long ago. She had been here before. There was a clump of trees which shaded the well. Richa didn't like the place much. There was something mysterious about it ... something unpleasant and scary. Bela knows the place well though, she thought. Why didn't Mrs Malhotra tell me about her?

Bela had already swarmed up one of the trees, a tall one with slender branches. Richa didn't know its name.

'Come on up,' she cried.

'No,' Richa said. 'I'm not very good at climbing trees.'

Actually, the only tree in the garden she could climb was a huge old mango tree with a low thick branch. She loved to sit on that, though.

'Darpok!' Bela cried. She scrambled down.

Suddenly she darted off again, while Richa, who wasn't a very fast runner, huffed behind her.

'Stop! Stop! Bela, where are you?' she cried. She couldn't see her any more. They were in sight of the house now. She could see her mother in the verandah.

'Richa!' she called out. 'It's time to drink your milk.'

Richa stopped. She looked around again, but Bela had vanished. She entered the house, frowning, dragging her steps. Couldn't she have told her that she was going? That girl, she really was strange. She was just about to tell her mother about her when she noticed that Mrs Malhotra was there. Suddenly, she felt hesitant. It was obvious that Mrs Malhotra had deliberately not told them about Bela. Was there some reason why she shouldn't be playing with her? She knew grown-ups had funny ideas sometimes. So, she decided to keep quiet.

She'll be my secret playmate, Richa thought. It seemed quite exciting to have one. Someone nobody knew anything about. So, when Bela came the next day, she didn't invite her into the house, but played with her in the garden. Bela seemed quite happy too that way. In fact, as time passed, somehow Richa got the feeling that Bela didn't want anyone to know that she was there.

One day, the mali had appeared suddenly while they were playing. To her surprise, Bela quickly ducked behind a bush. Only after he left, did she reappear.

'Why do you keep hiding?' Richa had asked irritably.

Bela just laughed in reply.

'Richa seems to have got used to being alone,' she heard Ma tell Papa one day. 'She spends all her time in the garden.'

'Thank God,' her father replied. 'I wasn't too sure if it was a good idea, staying so far from town.'

Richa felt a little guilty. She should have told them about Bela. But she couldn't somehow, just couldn't!

Instead, she wrote to Kavya, 'I have a new friend—Bela. We play together every afternoon. She's very adventurous. We have lots of fun ...' Actually, Bela was a little too adventurous. She was positively reckless. The way she swung from tree branches and leapt down from them as if nothing could happen to her!

'Come on,' she'd tell Richa. 'It's easy. Just try.'

'No thanks,' Richa would say. 'I'm happier on the ground. You're a real monkey. I'll get hurt if I try that.'

That always sent Bela off into fits of laughter. They did play quieter games, of course, like building a hut at the end of the garden, out of old bricks and fallen branches. They would sit there and play cards sometimes. But Richa had to teach Bela most of the games she knew.

'Where have you been living?' she asked her, one day. 'Don't they play these games here? I thought everybody knew them!'

Bela had giggled again, as if she were enjoying a private joke. But Richa had felt uneasy. Bela was so different. Different even from her school friends, girls who'd lived in this town all their lives. But she was such fun that Richa didn't want to put her off by asking awkward questions. She was quite likely to take off again and never return.

And then it happened. They were playing in the garden as usual, one afternoon, when she heard her mother's voice.

'Richa,' she called. Richa started and looked up, surprised to find her mother standing in front of her. Busy playing, she hadn't noticed her come.

'Who were you talking to?' There was a puzzled frown on her mother's face.

Mrs Malhotra was there too and the mali. Flustered, Richa blurted out, 'Bela, of course.' Her mother must have seen Bela, she thought. And actually, she was relieved. She didn't want to keep it a secret any longer.

'Bela? Who's that?' It was her mother's turn to look surprised. 'And where is she?'

'There—oh, she's run off again!' Richa cried out exasperated. 'I don't know why she does it. Hides all the time.'

All of a sudden, she heard a choked sound. It came from Mrs Malhotra. She'd gone white! And then her eyes fell on the mali's face. He looked terrified. Richa turned cold. What was wrong?

'Richa,' her mother said slowly. 'Are you sure you were talking to this ... this Bela? I was watching you. I didn't see anyone.' She turned to Mrs Malhotra. 'Did you?'

'N-no,' Mrs Malhotra's voice shook. She looked away. And as for the mali—he muttered something under his breath, picked up his tools and scurried off as if someone was chasing him.

'But –' Richa shivered suddenly, in spite of the steamy heat. She felt confused, befuddled.

It was as if there was a mist in front of her eyes. And then ... it cleared in a flash. She knew everything now! Why Bela could appear and reappear at will. Why she wore those funny clothes, spoke in that old-fashioned way. She wasn't real. She didn't live in the present. She'd lived long ago ... Yes, Bela was ... she was a ghost.

Strangely, she didn't feel scared. Just a little hurt that Bela hadn't told her. Well, she was a real prankster, wasn't she? Perhaps she thought it a great joke. Anyway, she'd catch her and tell her that she knew. And tell her also that it made no difference at all. They'd been friends all this time and there was no reason why they couldn't continue.

Mrs Malhotra left early that day. Richa wanted to laugh. Bela had really shaken everyone up. But her mother looked worried ... really worried. She glanced at Richa again and again. Richa felt uneasy.

Would she tell her to stop playing with Bela? No, she couldn't, she mustn't!

But it was obvious that she knew. Mrs Malhotra must have told her. They all knew about Bela, it seemed. Even the mali. What had he muttered under his breath as he fled? It sounded like, 'I told them not to plant bela ...' But why were they scared? Bela had never harmed anyone ...

That night at dinner, Papa said all of a sudden, 'Well, the company's got us a nice modern house—in the middle of town.' His voice sounded so false and hearty that Richa's heart began to sink. 'There'll be company for you there, Richa. Lots of children to play with. We'll move there right away.'

'No!' Richa screamed. Her voice sounded different. She could see her mother go pale. 'I like this house, Papa. I want to stay here. Please let's stay here. Please!'

She stopped when she saw her parents exchange glances. Papa knew too! Ma must have rung him up and told him. She got up from the table and ran to her room. Tears streamed from her eyes. The thought of going away, never meeting Bela again seemed unbearable. Why were they doing this to her? She switched off the light and lay down. Could she somehow persuade her father, convince him that Bela was harmless? But in her heart of hearts she knew she couldn't ...

When she fell asleep at last, she dreamt of Bela. They were playing by the well. Usually, Richa refused to go there, though Bela often tried to persuade her. 'Catch me!' Bela cried out. To Richa's surprise, she picked up the cover of the well and jumped in!

'Bela!' Richa screamed. 'Come out! Come out at once! Don't go away, Bela!'

And then ... she woke up sweating, her heart pounding like mad. The moon shone bright and cold through the window. There was something so sad, so gloomy about it. Just like that place by the well. She lay there, listening to her heart beat. It's too unfair, she thought. I always have to leave my friends behind. I don't want to leave Bela and go. I won't!

Then ... she realized that the thuk-thuk-thuk was not her heart beat—but someone tapping at the window. Richa sat up at once. She felt a sudden thrill. Goosebumps marched down her arms.

'Richa,' she heard a faint whisper. 'Come out ... Richa ... Ri-chaaa. It's lovely out here!'

Bela, she thought exultantly. Her whole body tingled. A horrible, restless feeling took hold of her. She wanted to rush out at once. Even a second's delay seemed painful.

'Come on, Richa. Hurry!' Bela whispered again. Her voice was smooth, beguiling. But there was an awful urgency underneath. 'We'll go play by the well. We'll have such fun, wait and see, such fun. And we'll always be together ...'

'Yes, yes!' Richa jumped out of bed. She hunted frantically for her slippers. 'I'm coming, Bela. Wait for me ... I'm coming.'

She shoved her feet into her slippers and ran to the window.

She opened the latch, was about to step out. And then—her mother's voice rang out, sharp and high, 'Where are you going, Richa?' Richa froze. Her bones seemed to melt. She heard the light switch click on, felt the sudden brightness sting her eyes.

'Nowhere, nowhere, Ma!' Richa's teeth chattered, she felt her heart shrink into a tight, hard ball.

'Come and sleep in my room!' Her mother's voice shook. She clutched Richa's arm.

Richa wanted to pull away. She wanted to throw herself out of the window. But her mother held her tightly. A huge sob tore at her chest. Her feet stumbled as her mother led her away. She thought of Bela waiting and waiting, thought of the wonderful games she wouldn't be able to play any more ...

They left the house the very next morning. 'Mrs Malhotra will get our stuff packed up and sent,' Ma said. Her eyes were red—her face looked tired—as if she hadn't slept all night. She looked at Richa again and again and she looked scared—no, terrified!

Richa hated the house as soon as she saw it. It was just a box, a concrete box. 'I don't want to stay here!' she cried out. 'I –'

'Hush, my dear,' her mother said, holding her close as she wept and wept. 'Don't, darling, don't. Wait and see, you'll love it here ... See, there's a girl there, in the house opposite. Maybe ... maybe you can be friends with her.'

Richa didn't want to look—but something seemed to tug at her eyes. She went to the window. The tall girl with two plaits trailing over her shoulders smiled and waved. Richa's heart flipped over. She felt as if she were floating ...

'Bela,' she mouthed.

FIRE!

'Sh-sh-sh,' whispered the pines. It was a warm summer afternoon. A heat haze hung in the air like an uncomfortable curtain, blotting out the distant hills.

Puja and Mitu were perched on the hillside, just at the edge of the patch of forest above Puja's house. 'Oh, what a lazy, lazy afternoon,' Puja sighed. She lay back, trying to ignore the pine needles pricking her back.

Through half-closed eyes she gazed at the house, the sloping red tin roof, the creepers winding up the verandah pillars. A thin blue spiral of smoke coiled up from the small outhouse below it, where Paruli stayed with her mother. Lower down the hill, she could see Mitu's house, a large squarish bungalow.

'Hey, isn't that Paruli's village?' Mitu cried, as though she'd picked up Puja's train of thought and carried it further. She pointed to a spot in a distant valley where the sunlight caught a slender, ribbon-like streamlet, turned it to silver and flashed on a cluster of slate-roofed houses. 'How close it looks! I can't believe it's ten miles away.'

Puja opened an eye. 'Mmm, yes,' she murmured.

Skinny and energetic, Mitu sprang to her feet to have a better look. Then she cried, 'Listen, aren't we going to try your new cooking things?' Nine-year-old Puja's aunt had brought her a set of small cooking utensils—a pressure cooker, a karahi and little cooking pots.

Puja wound a curl around her finger. 'Oh well, okay,' she said.

Mitu got busy. She laid out two big stones and piled twigs between them. 'This is our fire,' she pronounced. Gravely, she broke off some leaves into the karahi and set it on the make-believe fire.

'These are our vegetables,' she said. 'What are you going to make, Puja?'

'Can't I just eat?' Puja crinkled her short nose.

'Oh, you lump!' Mitu said disgustedly.

With a sigh, Puja sat up and stretched. Then something caught her eye. Someone had emerged from the outhouse and was scrambling up onto the wide path that led towards the forest.

'It's Paruli!' Puja was suddenly wide awake.

Mitu looked up. 'Strange,' she said. 'Generally, her mother keeps her quite busy working at this time.'

Paruli was the maid's daughter. At thirteen, she was much older than the other two but she loved to play with them, that is, when her mother allowed her a little time off. Paruli's mother firmly believed that girls were meant to be kept busy with household chores all the time.

The three had, in fact, become great pals. When Paruli had first come with her mother from the village, Puja and Mitu had found her a little odd. With her narrow kajaled eyes, her pierced nose, which had a black fern stem stuck in it to substitute for a nose ring and her faded hand-me-down clothes, she was different from their usual playmates. But once they came to know her better, they found her great fun because she was full of such adventurous ideas. She was the one who had discovered the place where the fattest, juiciest hisalu berries grew, crunchy orange cups that fell into your hand as soon as you touched them. She introduced them to the delights of roasted chana and mishri at the Shivratri fair and told them stories about the various birds that flew and chirped in the forest. With Paruli, they never knew what exciting activity was coming up next.

'Paroo-li!' Puja yelled out. Paruli waved back. 'Why doesn't she just come straight up?' Puja muttered impatiently, as Paruli meandered about the forest picking up twigs. Eventually, she reached the spot where they were sitting.

'What's cooking?' she asked. Inadvertently, she glanced towards the house as though she were scared that her mother might have seen her.

'What's the matter?' Mitu asked. 'Has your mother been yelling at you?'

Paruli's face was expressionless as she shook her head quickly. But both girls knew her mother had a quick temper, even hit her sometimes. Suddenly, Paruli put her bundle of twigs down. She bent to pick up a shiny cooking pot, a perfect copy of a real one. Her face lit up as she examined it. 'You could make a whole cup of tea in this!' she said.

'A cup of tea!' Puja exclaimed, excited.

'A cup of tea,' Mitu echoed.

'Yes ... shall we?' Paruli urged. 'We can get some tea leaves and milk from the kitchen.'

'But,' Puja said, 'we'll need a real fire!'

'A real fire!' Mitu's eyes glistened. 'But how? We don't have any matches!'

'I'll manage that,' Paruli said. She quickly picked up her bundle of twigs and scrambled down. 'I'll be back in just a minute,' she said.

'A real fire! Wow!' Mitu was breathless. 'I'll get some water.' She rushed to the little spring that lay in a damp hollow some distance away—the only one that didn't dry up in summer.

Eagerly, they waited. A real fire, real tea. Fancy that!

After a while, Paruli returned, climbing up the slope carefully. She had a little cloth bag slung over her shoulder and—in a pair of tongs she held—a real live glowing coal! 'I got it from the wood fire. Get some pine needles,' she called.

Even Puja's stubby legs moved fast as she scooped up heaps of dry pine needles. The pile of pine needles was placed carefully between the stones, on top of the twigs, the cooking pot nestled on top of them. Then Paruli dropped the coal on it. The sun-dried needles caught fire at once, tiny flames licked up around them, then grew and grew as they watched, fascinated.

Then ... Swoosh! The fire flared up wildly, tossing the little pot aside. It roared out beyond the stones as a gust of wind fanned the flames. The dry pine needles that carpeted the forest floor provided plenty of fuel.

The girls jumped up in a fright. Petrified, they watched the fire spreading, devouring bushes, reaching out to the tall trees.

Paruli was the first to come to her senses. 'Fire!' she cried, 'Run! Run!'

'Fire!' Puja yelped, practically tumbling down the hill. 'Fire! Fire!'

Their first thought was to get away from the threatening flames. But when they reached the wide path that led to Puja's house, they paused. How could they go home and say that they had set the forest on fire? They were both strictly forbidden to so much as light a matchstick!

Puja took the lead. She ran down the lower path that led to the orchard behind the house. Mitu followed, ignoring the track that would lead her homewards. They could hear Paruli yelling 'Fire! Fire!' as she ran towards the house for help, got a vague glimpse of figures rushing from the house, and heard shouts. When they reached the orchard they stopped, hearts pounding.

'What's going to happen now?' Mitu was almost in tears. 'Why did we ever agree to have a fire? I never thought it would spread like that.'

'Neither did I,' said Puja. She was still panting. 'I wonder what's happening ... It's all Paruli's fault. She was the one who brought the coal. I wonder how she dared to go home!'

But Mitu said distractedly, 'Suppose the fire reaches the house, suppose they can't control it! Oh, I'm so scared. It'll all be our fault.'

Shivering with fright they waited. The orchard was too far away from the forest—on the other side of the hill. They couldn't see what was happening from there. They could only wait in painful suspense, listening with all their might for any sound that might give them a clue, cowering under the fruit trees.

They waited and waited. Finally, sick of trying to guess what could have happened, Puja said, 'I think we should go back. I think they've put out the fire. It was only a small one.' She felt braver now, since nothing disastrous seemed to have occurred.

'Do you think so?' Mitu asked. 'I'm terrified. Everyone will be furious.'

'Well, it wasn't really our fault.' Puja reached out and broke a plum. It was pretty raw and made her mouth tingle with its sourness, but lunch had been hours ago and she was quite hungry. She'd just bitten into it when a rustling sound made her turn. It was Paruli.

'Paruli, what's happening?' Mitu burst out anxiously, grabbing her arm.

Paruli gave them a stern look, but it was her reply that really shocked them. 'Everyone's very angry with you,' she said. 'You did a very wrong thing, lighting a fire in the forest.'

Puja's mouth fell open. She was too stunned to say anything. Paruli's accusing tone quite took her breath away. Wasn't she the main culprit? Hadn't she suggested the fire and brought the lighted piece of coal?

But Mitu wailed, 'Oh, no!' And then, 'Is it all right now?'

'Yes! They managed to beat out the fire. It had spread really far though. We had a tough time controlling it.'

'But listen, Paruli ...' Puja said. She had recovered from the initial surprise and wanted an explanation.

'I'm going, my mother's calling me. Don't worry. I won't tell anyone you're here!' And Paruli rushed away.

Mitu began to cry. 'What'll we do now?'

Puja burst out angrily, 'What cheek! Putting all the blame on us!'

'Oh, oh why did we listen to her?' Mitu sobbed.

Puja bit into her plum furiously. The sun was slipping towards the horizon. Soon it would be dark. They couldn't hang around the orchard forever. And she was starving now. 'We have to go back some time,' she said. 'We might as well get it over with.'

Mitu hesitated, then she too nodded reluctantly. Slowly they crept up the path, up the worn stone steps that led to the house. The wind brought a whiff of smoke, the acrid smell of burning wood. With guilty fear they turned their eyes towards the forest and were shocked to see the charred tree trunks, a dismal sight even from this distance.

Puja's mother was sitting in the verandah. Silently they faced her, heads hung low in shame.

'So where have you been hiding all this time?' Her voice was unusually severe. 'Aren't you ashamed of yourselves?'

Mitu sniffed. But Puja looked straight into her mother's eyes. 'Ma,' she said. 'We're very sorry. We never realized that the fire would spread so fast.'

'Now you realize I hope,' Ma's voice was still hard. 'It was a very, very dangerous thing you did. You could have got badly burnt.'

'Ma,' Puja continued, 'it was not our fault. Paruli brought a piece of lighted coal—'

'But you asked me!' A high-pitched voice interrupted.

It was Paruli—gazing at them with an air of injured innocence.

'Asked you?' Puja gasped. 'What a lie! We never thought of a fire.'

'Is this true, Paruli?' Ma asked. Paruli didn't answer. Just stood there looking aggrieved.

'All right, all right,' Ma said finally. 'I hope you have all learned a lesson from this.'

'Yes, Ma,' Puja said, her voice subdued.

'Yes, aunty,' Mitu's voice could barely be heard.

Mitu was sent home. Puja drank her milk and sat brooding silently. How could Paruli have told such lies? She was the one who had suggested the fire.

'I'll never play with her again,' she muttered to herself. 'I won't even talk to her.'

And Puja kept her word. The next day she told Mitu what she'd decided and Mitu agreed wholeheartedly. They decided to boycott Paruli totally. When she turned up to play, looking as if nothing had happened, they acted as if she wasn't there at all. Since they'd been forbidden to go to the forest as a punishment, they played near the house.

Paruli watched, hovering uncertainly at a distance. She watched them build a little hut with walls of stone, roofed with twigs, with a real garden around it made of transplanted seedlings. After a while, she vanished.

'Thank God,' Puja said. 'I hate someone watching me play.'

'Yes,' Mitu said, 'it spoils all the fun.'

But that very moment Paruli reappeared. She held two branches covered with mauve jacaranda flowers. For a while she stood there as if waiting for someone to take them from her. When no one did, she came and began to plant them in the garden.

Puja jumped up at once. 'Let's go, Mitu,' she said, 'or we'll be blamed for spoiling the jacaranda trees. Some people love to get others in trouble.'

'L-look, l-listen,' Paruli began. But Puja ran away and Mitu followed. Paruli just stood there looking hurt and ashamed at the same time.

'What are we going to do today?' Mitu asked the next morning, when she came to play with Puja. They had watered their 'garden', added a plant or two. The day stretched before them, long and dull.

Puja shrugged.

'Puja,' Mitu said cautiously, 'shall we make up with Paruli? It was terrible of her to blame us, but you know ...'

'Never!' Puja cried. 'I'll never make up with that liar. You can play with her if you want, but then, I won't play with you!'

'Okay, okay,' Mitu said placatingly. 'I thought maybe ...'

'Definitely not. Come, let's play cards. It's too hot outside in any case.'

They went inside and settled down to play cards. After a while, Mitu said, 'I was thinking, wondering why Paruli put all the blame on us. Maybe she was scared.'

'We were scared too,' Puja said. 'We also got into trouble.'

'But Puja, she's a servant,' Mitu said. 'And her mother—you know what she's like!'

'That doesn't mean that she should tell lies and put all the blame on us.' Puja's lower lip stuck out stubbornly. Mitu gave up then. She knew how hard it was to make Puja change her mind.

Two days passed. Puja continued to ignore Paruli. Then, one evening her mother said, 'Puja, I noticed that you are not talking to Paruli.'

'I don't feel like it, Ma.'

'But you were almost inseparable before.'

Puja remained silent. She knew her mother was right. They had been inseparable—Puja, Mitu and Paruli. But Paruli had let them down, betrayed their friendship.

'Darling ... you should be more forgiving,' her mother said gently.

'I've forgiven her,' Puja said. 'But do I have to play with her?'

Her mother sighed and turned away, saying, 'I hope that after some time you will forget and really forgive.'

A few days later, Puja went to play at Mitu's house. Mitu's mother took them for a long walk to the riverside. They carried a picnic lunch with them. When they got back, it was late afternoon.

'Puja,' Ma said. 'Paruli was looking for you.'

'Whatever for?' Puja frowned. But inside she felt a surge of excitement. Actually, she was ready to make up with Paruli now. Their games felt tame and childish without her. But she didn't know how to make the first move.

'Her father had come,' Ma went on, 'to take her back to the village. She went with him.'

'So—' Puja tried to sound indifferent, in spite of her sudden feeling of dismay. 'She'll come back, won't she?'

'I'm not sure. Her father wants to marry her off.'

'Paruli—married!' Puja was aghast. 'Ma, why didn't you stop them? She's not old enough to be married. How can they?'

'I tried, dear. But they just wouldn't listen. Her father was quite adamant. Her mother is also taking leave in a few days.'

'Oh-h ...' Puja just didn't know what to say. This strange turn of events utterly confounded her. It sounded impossible and ridiculous.

'She just wanted to say goodbye,' Ma ended.

'Oh-h ...' Puja's face grew longer. 'Won't she ever come back now?'

'I'm sure she will. But probably for a very short visit.'

Puja turned away silently. She went and sat under the cypress tree. A terrible feeling of loss gripped her. Suddenly she thought of Paruli slashing away the stinging nettles from their paths, on one of their excursions to the forest, so they wouldn't touch them by mistake and suffer. Picking up thorny branches and casting them aside ... and then ... standing hesitantly with the jacaranda branches in her hand.

Mitu was right. She had told lies because she was scared. Because she could get into much worse trouble than them. Why couldn't I understand, Puja thought? We were friends, weren't we? And now she had lost the chance to make up ...

Many months later, Paruli came for a visit. An older and subdued Paruli, who hardly spoke to Puja. In fact, she hardly spoke at all. Getting married seemed to have thrown her into a permanent state of embarrassment. She was busy helping in the kitchen most of the time. Or she sat outside trying to knit something from a much-unravelled ball of wool.

'Paruli,' Puja wanted to say. 'It's all forgiven and forgotten. Let's make up and be friends again. Let's have fun like we used to.'

But she knew it was too late. Because Paruli was not their playmate Paruli any longer. She had entered the world of grown-ups.

THE TOUGH DECISION

The winter sunshine spread gently over the playground. It was break time at Green Valley School and girls were scattered all over—running around, practising shots on the basketball court or just sitting and munching on their tiffins.

A group hung around near the large open-air stage, the pride of the school. They were listening intently to a wavy-haired girl, standing in the centre.

'I'll be wearing this lovely white dress, you know, made of net, with silver sequins all over—'

'Wow!'

'And,' she continued, fluttering her eyelashes, 'there'll be a gold crown on my head.'

A murmur of admiration rose from the bunch. The girl, whose name was Akanksha, smiled with satisfaction.

But there was someone else who was not so impressed. It was a plump girl, with short cropped hair and she had a disgusted frown on her face. 'Chhee!' she screwed up her short, broad nose. 'What a show-off!'

'Gauri!' exclaimed her companion in surprise, a small, quiet-looking girl. 'What's the matter with you?'

'Well, Manavi, I'm quite fed up of dear Akky's airs. She seems to think she's another Deepika Padukone!'

'Just ignore her,' Manavi replied. 'It's not worth getting worked up about.'

Gauri and Manavi were known to be inseparable, even though the two were so different that people wondered at their friendship. Gauri was blunt and outspoken and never bothered to mince her words, while Manavi was so quiet that people hardly ever heard her voice.

Akanksha flung an unpleasant look at them. They were standing too far for her to have heard

Gauri's remark, but she had probably guessed from her expression that it was nothing complimentary to her. The two were long standing rivals.

Just then the bell rang for class and the playground emptied rapidly. Only the group by the stage remained because they were waiting to rehearse a play.

Soon Mrs Bhalla came bustling along. She was the elocution teacher and a talented dramatics coach. Tall, with a pleasant, open face, the students loved her direct, informal manner, which was so different from that of the other teachers.

'So!' she said briskly. 'You look eager to begin.' She paused, flashing them a broad smile. '*A Midsummer Night's Dream* is a delightful play—though we're only doing a few scenes. But I'm sure you can do justice to Shakespeare, now that you're more experienced.'

'Oh, ma'am,' Akanksha rolled her large eyes and said with a syrupy smile, 'We're just dying to start!'

'Good,' Mrs. Bhalla replied in her no-nonsense manner, unmoved by her flattering tone. 'You've already been given your parts, so shall we read? By the way we're lucky to have two excellent roles for our two outstanding actors. Titania is just right for Akanksha and I'm sure Gauri will be perfect as Bottom, with her flair for comedy. And yes, Rina, you're nice and tall. I think you'll make a good Oberon.'

The girls jumped on to the stage and the rehearsal began in real earnest.

This was the very first time Manavi was taking part in a play. It was a small role—she was Peaseblossom, one of the fairies waiting on Queen Titania. Still, she was thrilled about it, though Gauri had had to really get after her to try acting.

'You'll feel more confident about speaking up,' she had said.

Manavi had agreed reluctantly and now when her turn came, she was sorry she had. She felt just like a block of wood.

But Mrs Bhalla smiled encouragingly. 'Don't worry,' she said. 'You'll be surprised at yourself when the real day arrives.'

Manavi smiled back shyly though she was not so sure. She thought of the video recording of the play Mrs Bhalla had shown them—by a famous theatre group. How scintillating it had been!

Because right now, even Akanksha and Gauri didn't seem able to put life into their parts.

'Come on, Titania, show some affection,' Mrs Bhalla called out. 'You're supposed to be in love!'

'She'd have to be a *really* good actress to do that,' Gauri muttered.

Akanksha's smile grew fixed though she didn't speak. The period ended just then, luckily, and the rehearsal broke up.

Chattering excitedly, the girls hurried to the next class. Akanksha, as usual, was surrounded by her 'chamchis'.

'Why did you say that?' Manavi whispered to Gauri. 'You know Akanksha. She'll say you're jealous.'

'Me—jealous?' Gauri retorted. 'I'm a much better actress—even though she always manages to steal the prize.'

'Gauri! What's happening to you?' Manavi said, troubled. 'Don't let her get to you!'

Manavi had known her friend for a long time but she had never seen this vindictive streak. 'Anyway,' she continued. 'You have a terrific role. You're sure to win the prize this time.'

'I'm not so sure,' Gauri's face clouded, 'though it's tailor-made for me. But the judges seem to go for glamour, not talent.'

At the next rehearsal, the following day, Manavi could sense a slight change. The girls were beginning to get a feel for their parts, though it was still far from perfect.

'*...and thy fair virtue's force perforce doth move me*
On the first view, to say, to swear, I love thee.'

Akanksha sounded more convincing now.

'*Methinks, mistress, you should have little reason for that ...*' said Gauri as Bottom in a matter-of-fact way.

'She's absolutely right,' one of the chamchis nudged another and giggled. 'Isn't it funny,' she whispered. 'Akanksha having to pretend to be crazy about Gauri!'

The chamchis always would accompany Akanksha to the rehearsals though they were not in the play.

'Yeah!' smirked another. 'But what fantastic acting!'

Manavi heard them as she waited for her cue. Personally, she thought Akanksha didn't have to act. She was just being herself as Titania—vain, wilful and spiteful.

The chamchis would always clap loudly when Akanksha delivered her lines and she would smile making Gauri frown.

'It's too sickening,' she said later. 'They only clap for her. As if the rest of us can't act.'

'Just ignore them,' Manavi said reassuringly. 'You're doing a wonderful job. That funny expression of yours—I almost burst out laughing on stage.'

But Gauri couldn't ignore them. She stuck it out through the next rehearsal, then went and complained to Mrs Bhalla.

'Hmmm,' Mrs Bhalla nodded. 'I'm not too happy about those girls being there either. But I said nothing because no one seemed to mind.'

So, when Akanksha sailed in with her entourage the next day, she got a big shock.

'Only people acting in the play will remain please,' Mrs Bhalla said crisply. 'We don't need an audience for the rehearsals. It disturbs everyone.'

Akanksha's face flamed with anger as the chamchis filed out sulkily. She cast a venomous glance at Gauri, as though she could guess who was behind it.

'Thanks, ma'am,' the other actors spoke up. 'They were a nuisance. We don't want an audience till we're perfect.'

Akanksha went almost purple, but she controlled herself and said with an ingratiating smile, 'I'm so sorry, ma'am. My silly friends insisted on coming and watching me act.'

This was their first rehearsal without using their books and it went off perfectly. Since they had learnt the lines for their parts, the delivery sounded more natural now. Also, they could move about and gesture more freely. Manavi felt that the chamchis not being there made a big difference too!

At the end of the rehearsal, Mrs Bhalla announced, 'Girls, I'm thinking of entering the play in the Inter-School Drama competition. I think we stand a good chance.'

Everyone cheered and the next day they rehearsed with even greater enthusiasm. Manavi found it fascinating, the way the play shaped up. Of course, there were lapses still. People forgot their lines, sometimes missed their cues. But Mrs Bhalla was quite happy with the way it was going and so were the girls.

And then, something not so nice happened. Manavi had just entered class when she heard one of the chamchis say, 'Have you heard? Mrs Bhalla has gone on leave.' 'Who'll direct the play?' another asked.

The question was left hanging because Mrs Kapoor, their English teacher, entered just then. Manavi's heart sank. 'I hope it's not true,' she thought. Then, Akanksha got up and offered some lovely roses to the teacher, who was new to the school, saying, 'From my garden, ma'am.'

An uneasy suspicion formed in Manavi's mind. Was Mrs Kapoor going to fill in for Mrs Bhalla? But how would Akanksha know that?

Sure enough, when they went for their rehearsals, Mrs Kapoor arrived. 'Mrs Bhalla's quite sick, girls, and will be away for some time,' she said. 'I'll fill in for her.'

The girls' faces fell. They were sorry for Mrs Bhalla but sorry for themselves too. They had come to depend on her so much.

Glumly they positioned themselves on the stage. Suddenly Gauri noticed that the chamchis were back in full force!

'Ma'am,' she burst out, 'these girls are not supposed to be here!'

'Why not?' Akanksha asked aggressively. 'I think,' she said, turning to Mrs Kapoor with a winning smile, 'it'll help us to know the audience reaction.'

Mrs Kapoor hesitated for a moment. But perhaps Gauri's brusque tone had annoyed her. 'Let them stay,' she said.

The chamchis behaved perfectly for a couple of days. But soon they went back to their old ways. They yawned loudly when Gauri delivered her lines and looked obviously bored at her antics. Once, they even walked out pointedly. Gauri tried to tolerate it, till the day they went too far.

It was the scene when Titania comes back to her senses and realizes she's in love with a donkey.

'My Oberon! What visions have I seen!

Methought, I was enamour'd of an ass,'

Akanksha said with great feeling.

'Ha! Ha!' laughed the chamchis. 'She's absolutely right,' one of them whispered loudly.

Gauri was furious. Somehow, she controlled herself at that point but she let fly when she and Manavi were by themselves. 'I've had it!' she fumed. 'I'm not attending any more rehearsals.'

'You can't do that!' Manavi cried. 'There's just one week left for the show. And can't you see? That's just what Akanksha wants—to push you out, make you look bad.'

Gauri looked thoughtful then. She nodded, but the way her mouth set a moment later made Manavi uneasy. Was she planning to retaliate in some way?

After the dress rehearsal, she dropped her bombshell. It had been a chaotic affair. People had muffed their lines, one fairy's wings had dropped off, reducing her to tears. Gauri's own acting had been mechanical and uninspired.

But as they trooped out gloomily, a familiar voice said, 'That was awful, wasn't it?'

'Mrs Bhalla!' They rushed to surround her. 'Thank God you're okay!'

'Never mind,' she said. 'A bad dress rehearsal means a good final performance.'

Later, as they were taking off their make-up in the green room, Akanksha was holding court as usual, gorgeous in her costume. Gauri was watching her. Suddenly a broad smile transformed her sullen face.

Manavi wondered what had brought about the change. But when Gauri told her, she was horrified.

'You can't be serious,' she said, aghast. 'It'll be a disaster.'

'I am and I will do it,' Gauri said stubbornly.

'But-but the school play will be ruined! We'll lose the prize!'

'Don't you dare talk to me about prizes,' Gauri walked off in a huff.

But Manavi couldn't help brooding over Gauri's outrageous plan. It was a simple one. Akanskha happened to be terrified of lizards and Gauri happened to have two brothers addicted to practical jokes. Gauri planned to borrow a plastic lizard from them, which looked horrifyingly real, and drop it on Akanksha's lap in the course of the play.

'She'll make a real fool of herself, screaming and hopping about in that silly white dress she was bragging about!' Gauri had said exultantly.

'What should I do?' Manavi thought, almost frantic. There was hardly any time to think—the play was the very next day. She could hardly warn Akanksha or tell Mrs Bhalla. It would mean betraying her friend and that was too awful to even think about. But neither would Gauri see reason.

Should she just let her go ahead with her plan—but ... the play meant so much, they had worked so hard. Gauri's friendship meant a great deal to Manavi too. What was she to do!

Then, the big day arrived and they were in the green room struggling into their costumes and applying make-up. Squeals and cries came from every corner. 'Hey, this doesn't fit!' 'Pass me a pin, please ... CAN someone pass me a pin?' 'God, don't I look a perfect clown?' And so on.

Gauri was in high spirits, laughing and joking even with Akanksha who looked absolutely stumped at this change. But Manavi was so tense that she felt she would snap. Not only was it her first stage appearance—but—she still didn't know what she should do!

Just before the play, the solution came to her. It was a very tough decision to make, but ... she knew she had to do it. It took all she had to persuade herself—

because there would be a huge price to pay ... She had never opposed Gauri before. In anything at all! She always been the 'Yes' girl. But ... not this time ...

The stage looked like a real fairyland, with trees and plants placed here and there to transform it into a forest. Softly glowing lights gave an impression of moonlight.

The play took off, right from the start. The long hours of rehearsal paid off now, each and every one excelled in their parts. But Gauri as Bottom easily stole the show. Her buffoonery had everyone rolling with laughter.

Manavi was keeping an anxious eye on her. Then the scene came when Bottom reposed on Titania's lap with the fairies flitting around them. Only Manavi caught Gauri's swift movement. Before she could direct Akanksha's attention to the thing on her lap, Manavi darted forward and grabbed it. Akanksha was startled, but Gauri looked absolutely furious. Being good actors, they quickly recovered and went on. Nobody even noticed what had happened.

'What do you think you were doing?' Akanksha lashed out at her when the scene ended. 'Trying to throw me off? Jealous cat!'

Manavi bit her lip and remained silent. If only Akanksha knew!

But the look Gauri gave her was much more disturbing. Manavi gulped and sniffed down the tears that were rising to her eyes.

Then the play was over, to deafening applause. Theirs was the last one. Quickly, Manavi slipped out of her costume. Then, as she turned to go she came face to face with Gauri.

'You stupid fool,' she hissed. 'Why did you do that?'

'I did what I had to,' Manavi said quietly. 'I couldn't allow you to let us all down like that. Yourself too. It would have been terrible.'

'*You* let me down!' Gauri said angrily. 'I thought you were my friend!'

'Don't tell me the two inseparables are fighting,' someone said. It was Mrs Bhalla.

'Oh no, ma'am,' Manavi tried to cover up.

'You were both wonderful, girls,' Mrs Bhalla smiled. 'I'm really proud of you all.'

'Thanks, ma'am,' they said mechanically.

For a moment they stood there in awkward silence. Then Mrs Bhalla said, 'Don't leave before the judges' decision. It'll be any moment now.'

Stiffly, without looking at each other, they walked into the auditorium packed with noisy school children, and sat down.

As the judges stood up to announce their verdict, an expectant hush fell over the hall.

'The prize for the best play goes to ... *A Midsummer Night's Dream*!'

They were on their feet, yelling, clapping. Gauri turned to Manavi, her frown had vanished and there was a big grin on her face as she hugged her. 'We did it! We did it!' she cried.

In their excitement, they barely heard the other prizes being announced till Manavi's ears caught something.

'Listen!' she clutched Gauri's arm. 'They're saying something. Your name Gauri—you've won the Best Actress award!'

Gauri looked stunned and unbelieving. All her schoolmates were turning around to cheer and shake her hand so hard that it looked they might pull it right off!

'At last,' she said, finally, squeezing Manavi's hand. 'Thanks to you!'

Manavi's eyes glistened with unshed tears. Then she straightened her back and let out a deep sigh. What a tough decision it had been ...

WHY ME?

Kanav was stomping down the corridor, his mood as foul as it could possibly be, when the whirring sound of wheels made him halt in his tracks. It was the wheelchair boy. He was racing along at an unimaginable speed. Kanav stopped, a little alarmed. Was the wheelchair out of control? At this rate the boy would be hurled to the end of the corridor and go tumbling down the steps that led into the school garden. He had to stop him. Without pausing to think twice, he dived at the rushing wheelchair and grabbed it. His body was jerked so hard that he fell. His arms felt like they were almost pulled out of their sockets, but the wheelchair came to a standstill.

The boy stared at him open mouthed. To Kanav's surprise, he didn't look either relieved or thankful. For a moment Kanav didn't know what to say. Had he made a mistake?

Then the boy cleared his throat and said, 'Thanks so much ... for trying to help, but my wheelchair was not running away with me.' His eyes had a merry twinkle as he continued, 'You see, I'm practising for the wheelchair race.'

'Oh ... I'm sorry.' Kanav felt rather sheepish.

'It's okay,' the boy smiled. 'But I think we're getting late for class.'

'Oh yes!' Kanav jumped up.

He was still a little breathless when they entered the classroom. Ms Kumar, their teacher frowned. 'You're late, Kanav,' she said disapprovingly.

'Ma'am, he was trying to help me,' said the boy quickly. 'My wheelchair developed a snag.'

'Oh ... I'm glad to hear you were helpful, Kanav.' Ms Kumar raised her eyebrows in surprise.

Kanav flushed. Ms Kumar didn't like him, he knew. He was hardly teacher's pet material—disruptive in class, whispering at the back, eating chocolate, passing notes. As he mouthed, 'Thanks,' to the boy, he noticed that Nihar and Virat exchanged a puzzled glance.

Did they also think that it was unlike him to help? His closest friends, today they had irritated him all through break by going on and on about all the exciting places they had visited during their summer holidays.

Kanav had no choice but to listen, pretending to be interested even though he was feeling terribly left out. Then Nihar said, 'It must have been a real bore boiling in the heat here in Delhi, Kanav.' He was trying to be sympathetic perhaps, but it made Kanav feel worse.

'Oh, but you were planning to join all kinds of workshops, weren't you?' Virat had added quickly.

'Yes, yes, I was.' Kanav had tried to smile but suddenly he couldn't bear it any longer. 'Guys, I just need to use the washroom,' he mumbled and walked away rapidly, mopping his streaming face.

The July heat was oppressive, but the first day in school after the summer holidays had become more of an ordeal than he could have imagined.

He rushed into the first vacant stall, banged it shut and stood there choking on his tears. Why had this happened? Why had his dad bungled up so badly?

Last year he had been swapping stories about the family trip to the US and his visit to Disneyland and Grand Canyon and Niagara Falls. This year, all he could do was listen to the others go on. The worst was the thought ... if his friends found out that his father had had massive losses in business and they were in dire financial straits, would they treat him the same as before?

It was bad enough that the usual fun holiday had to be forfeited. Though he was twelve years old, he had cried like a baby when his mother told him that they needed to sell the house and move to a smaller place.

His life was falling apart, and it was all his father's fault.

'This is only temporary, beta,' Dad had said, putting an arm around his shoulder. 'I promise, soon things will be back to normal.'

Temporary! Why did it need to happen at all?

'Kanav Chandra, I asked you a question!' Ms Kumar's sharp voice sliced away his reverie. 'Who won the First Battle of Panipat?'

'Umm, yes, ma'am,' Kanav sat up straight. His heart thumped. For the life of him, he couldn't remember. Then he felt a finger poking his side, 'Babar,' someone whispered. 'Uh-uh, Babar, ma'am,' Kanav repeated after a short pause. He felt awkward, but a dressing down from the teacher would be the end.

'Hmm ...' Ms Kumar pursed her lips. 'No more daydreaming now.'

When he could escape her eye, Kanav glanced back surreptitiously. The wheelchair boy smiled and winked. Kanav smiled back. He hadn't noticed that he sat behind him.

The period ended and Kanav turned to thank him. 'You saved my life, yaar,' he said.

'Sajal,' said the boy, 'I'm Sajal. You tried to save mine too, remember?'

Kanav laughed and suddenly his mood lifted.

Sajal had joined the school just this term. Kanav and the others had kind of avoided him. Not that they weren't sympathetic, but they felt a little uncomfortable around him. Recalling how Sajal spent most of his break trundling his wheelchair up and down the smoother portions of the playground, a twinge of guilt knifed Kanav. How did it feel to be stuck like that when the rest of them were racing around, kicking balls and wrestling in fun? But why was he in a wheelchair? Was it from birth or had something happened to him?

Whatever it was, Kanav decided that he would try to be friendlier.

Returning home to the small flat they lived in now was depressing. They had had to let go of their maid, though thankfully their old cook whom Kanav called Ramesh Dada was still with them. He was waiting at the bus stop to receive Kanav.

'Your Ma had to go out,' he said, examining Kanav's face closely.

'Where?' Kanav wanted to ask, but decided not to. It was probably about a job.

Ma used to volunteer at an NGO, now she was looking for a job to contribute to their income. 'I've been working pretty hard,' she had said cheerfully. 'I think I should find something that pays me for my time.'

His father's face had acquired that beaten, hangdog expression that Kanav had come to hate when she said this.

Ma had tried to keep their spirits up throughout. But Kanav couldn't help but overhear his parents arguing when all this began. An awful sick feeling would come over him. Where had their happy family life vanished? And the disloyal thought would creep into his head ... it was all Dad's fault. He tried his best to block it, but it was impossible at times.

Ramesh Dada had cooked his favourite kadhi and rice today, mildly spicy with the sour tang of curd adding its flavour. The only problem was, with all that was going on, Kanav couldn't enjoy anything.

Come on, grow up, life is full of ups and downs, he tried to tell himself. But the thought, 'Why me?' grabbed hold of him again. Why me? Why me?

He shook his head wildly to lose it, and his eye fell on his school bag. Homework! He groaned. The last thing he needed to snap out of the blues. He was reaching for his iPad to play a game when suddenly, it struck him that he ought to do it for his mother. She was always after him to pay more attention to his studies. He had never taken her seriously.

Ma had enough to cope with. She would be overjoyed to find that he had done his homework without any nagging. As he opened his history book, he thought of Sajal and smiled. Tomorrow he would not need anyone to prompt him to answer a question in class.

At break the next day, Virat asked him as they were strolling out of class, 'What have you brought for tiffin? I have this fantastic quiche from this new French pastry shop.'

Kanav shrugged. 'Today, I just felt like a good old cheese sandwich,' he said.

'How boring!' Nihar wrinkled his nose. 'Don't tell me your fantastic Ramesh Dada has left?'

A hot flush burned Kanav's face. 'No, he's very much there. Why would he leave?'

It was Nihar's turn to shrug. There was a loud roaring in Kanav's ears. Why did Nihar say that? How much he had longed to confide his troubles in his friends! But he had hesitated, wondering how they would react. Now he felt relieved he hadn't.

At the far end of the field he saw Sajal trundling along. A thought nipped at him. 'I-I borrowed something from Sajal,' he said suddenly. 'I need to return it.'

'Sajal?' Nihar wrinkled his brow. 'How come you've suddenly become so pally with him?'

'Umm ... we're both in the chess club,' Kanav replied hurriedly.

It was true. They were both in the chess club,

though Kanav had never spoken to him there. Sajal was really good. Kanav had joined only because his parents felt he should have more interests.

'Practising for your wheelchair race?' Kanav smiled as he caught up with Sajal.

Sajal laughed. 'Yes, but I need someone to time me.'

'I can do that,' Kanav offered immediately, delighted he could do something for him.

'Who is this Sajal ... a new friend?' his mother asked that evening.

'Yes, but how do you know?' Kanav wrinkled his brow.

'You know our mothers' WhatsApp group? His mom sent me a message,' Ma replied. 'She's invited you to come over on Saturday to play chess. Do you want to go?'

'Of course! He's a wonderful guy ... he-he's in a wheelchair ... but always so cheerful ...' A nagging thought began to bother Kanav. He pushed it aside.

The next day at break he didn't wait for anyone, just followed Sajal out. 'Are we playing chess on Saturday?' he asked.

Sajal's eyes turned wary. 'If you feel like,' he said expressionlessly. Then he dropped his gaze. 'I'm sure you have more exciting things to do.'

'What can be more exciting than playing chess with the champion?' Kanav laughed. 'I know I'll lose each and every game. But I might pick up some tips.'

A broad smile stretched Sajal's face. 'See you then.'

Ma dropped him off at Sajal's. As he rang the bell, all of a sudden, he felt a little uncertain. He didn't know Sajal that well. Why had he jumped to accept the invitation? He wasn't that crazy about chess. And he had never been the do-gooder type.

'Oh ... Kanav, I presume?' The moment he met Sajal's mother, he realized from whom he got that merry smile. 'Come let me take you to his room. He's been over the moon since you agreed.'

Kanav felt warm all over. No one had ever made him feel so important.

The chess board was already laid out. Sajal was examining it intently when Kanav entered. 'Hi!' he grinned, 'Ms Kumar would be impressed with your punctuality!'

Kanav laughed. 'You did save my life that day,' he said, pulling up a chair.

'Like you saved mine!' Sajal replied, laughing.

'Please, yaar! You can't imagine how dumb I felt when I realized,' Kanav said sheepishly.

'Forget it, yaar! You were trying to help,' Sajal said. 'So, should we feed our tummies so our brains work better for the game?'

'Don't know how much difference it'll make to mine,' Kanav shrugged, 'but I never refuse a good offer of food.'

As Sajal's mother entered with a tray full of goodies, Kanav quickly rose to take it from her.

And then ... his eye fell on a photograph on the wall. He froze. It was Sajal. Climbing up an enormous rock, as normal as anyone else. Suddenly he became conscious of a peculiar silence weighing the room. Hurriedly, he tore his eyes away, as embarrassed as if he had uncovered an awkward secret.

Sajal's mother had turned white.

Slowly, Kanav put the tray down on a table. 'Sajal,' he said softly, 'shall I pass you a slice of pizza?' He tried to sound natural, though his throat felt completely clogged.

He started when Sajal called out in an unnaturally shrill voice, 'Mom! I told you to take down that photo! Take it down! Please ... take it down.'

Kanav didn't know where to look. He hadn't bargained for this. The thought flashed through his mind again—he didn't really know Sajal that well.

His mother stood there, rooted to the spot, her shoulders shaking. Then Kanav reached out and took the photo off the wall with trembling hands.

'Is that better?' he whispered.

Sajal's mother turned around and left the room abruptly.

'Can it ever be better?' Sajal yelled. Then to Kanav's horror, he dissolved into a fit of sobbing.

Kanav sat there, head bowed, till he heard Sajal say in a small voice, 'Pass me a tissue, please.'

Kanav passed him a tissue. Then he hesitantly picked up a glass of watermelon juice and gave it to him without speaking. 'I'm sorry,' he heard Sajal say hoarsely. 'If-if you want to go home, I'll understand. Don't know what came over me.'

Kanav drew a deep breath. 'Don't be silly,' he replied. 'Why would I want to go home? I've come to see if I can beat you at chess. It may take me a hundred visits, but I'm not going to give up.'

A faint smile split Sajal's face and Kanav felt as if a heavy load had slipped from his shoulders. It was after Kanav had lost two games that Sajal told him his story.

How it was a car accident that had injured him so badly that the doctors said he was not likely to walk again. How much Sajal had loved rock climbing and other sports. He didn't say how much he missed all that now, but it was obvious in his voice. In a whisper, he added at the end how his father had never forgiven himself, because he was the one driving. 'But how can I ever blame him?' he said. 'It was the other guy who crashed into us.'

Kanav flushed when he heard this, thinking how much he blamed his own father.

'I couldn't bear to go back to the same school,' Sajal said finally. 'I couldn't bear the thought that all my friends would pity me. Here everyone ignores me, and that feels much better.'

'Don't you dare say that,' Kanav shot back. 'It's not better. What about me? I don't ignore you! I dare not. Who will prompt me in Ms Kumar's class otherwise?'

Sajal roared with laughter.

It was the best sound Kanav had heard for a long, long time. Some day, he thought, he would tell Sajal his own story and how after meeting him, the words 'Why me?' had vanished from his mind. As well as the words, 'It's all Dad's fault.'

GREENCHICKENPOXITIS

'But I *don't* want to talk to her even!' Samira yelled. Her square face turned a deep beetroot red and her thick eyebrows drew together angrily.

'Shush,' Ma said. 'That's not nice. One has to be friendly towards guests, to people who come to visit you.'

'Guest!' Samira spat. 'But I didn't invite her.'

'But we did, darling,' Ma's voice was heavy with patience. Samira guessed that she was close to breaking point. 'Be reasonable, sweetie. Be nice.'

NICE! Samira sighed, or huffed rather. She hated that word. She jolly well knew why she had to be nice. Vanya's father was important. He could—well, he could do all sorts of things. Papa and Ma had to be nice to him and Vanya's mother. And—she had to be nice to that brat Vanya. She wanted to puke.

'I'm not! I'm not going to be nice!' she repeated to herself defiantly—but in her heart of hearts she knew she would. She couldn't spoil things for Papa like that. If only ...

Spots! The idea struck her that morning as she was looking at herself in the mirror while brushing her teeth. She smiled ... it would fun ... real fun ...

'Hi!' Even Vanya's voice was irritating. High pitched, nasal, it went right through your head. 'Why are you hiding in here? Scared of me?'

Even though she kept her back turned, Samira could imagine the sickening grin that must be splitting her face. The worst was Vanya *knew*! She knew that Samira had to be nice to her. 'Hey! What *is* wrong with you?'

This was the cue Samira had been waiting for! She swung around dramatically. Let Vanya get the full impact of the green spots painted on her face!

'Eeeeks! What's wrong with you!' Vanya's high pitched voice was shriller than ever. Her large popping eyes almost burst out of their sockets.

'Greenchickenpoxitis!' Samira said gravely. 'It's a very rare disease. And–' she lowered her voice meaningfully, 'it's highly infectious too.'

'No-o!' Vanya wailed. 'Why - why didn't your mom warn me?'

'She-she must have thought it might look rude–that–that you might think I didn't want to play with you ...'

'As if that could ever happen.' Vanya's confidence bounced back. Yes, the brat knew. 'Is–are they painful?'

'Horribly! They even come up inside your mouth. You can't eat. Want to see?' Samira knew how fond of eating Vanya was.

'No-o!' Vanya put a hand on top of her eyes, just in case Samira insisted on showing her. Of course, she wouldn't have. She hadn't painted any spots inside her mouth, naturally. 'Well ... I'm going. I suppose I might as well go and get bored with the oldies ... Hmm ... I might pick up some juicy gossip ...'

Samira could have hugged herself. Vanya turned. She was going ... going. Samira was just holding back her chuckle of delight ... when suddenly Vanya whirled around.

'You know ...' she said slowly. 'It might not be such a bad idea to catch it—even if it's as horrible as you say. I've some tests coming up next week. And after that an awful cousin of mine is coming to stay. I'd do anything to put *her* off. By the way—does it travel through the air or do I have to actually touch you?'

Samira held her breath. 'No, no! You don't want to catch it. It's really horribly, terribly painful. You don't know what you're letting yourself in for!' she said almost pleadingly. 'And ... suppose ... suppose your mom blames me for giving it to you?'

'Who cares!' Vanya's grin was infuriating. 'Hmm ... I think I'd better touch you just to make sure.'

'Stay away—' Samira screamed.

But Vanya was already reaching out. Samira froze as she felt her hard hand on her cheek. What would happen now? The paint would spread, or just wipe off. She closed her eyes tightly ... she could imagine the scene. The yells, screams, accusations and the dressing down that would follow. Oh, why, oh why did she do this crazy thing!

Then ... 'Greenchickenpoxitis ...' she heard Vanya say or rather squeal. 'Greenchickenpoxitis! It's brilliant, absolutely brilliant. And instantly catching. See—I've already got it!'

Samira opened a cautious eye. The green paint—it was smeared all over Vanya's hands.

She was about to groan aloud when she heard Vanya chuckle delightedly. 'To think I always thought you were such a stuck-up old thing. In fact, I just hated the thought of coming here and being forced to play with you. Hey ... how did you get the idea?'

Samira's eyes popped. She—stuck-up! She felt a wave of fury go over her. She wanted to slap

Vanya. But the very next minute she found herself exploding into laughter. She laughed so much that tears ran down her cheeks, leaving green streaks on her face.

Vanya joined in too.

'Greenchickenpoxitis ...' Vanya repeated dreamily when they finally stopped. 'Which paint did you use? And—do you think it might fool my mom?'

'I doubt it ...' Samira said. She began to wipe her face with a wet towel. 'But you could try it on your cousin ... who knows what might happen?'

'Hmmm ... who knows?' Vanya sounded thoughtful.

The very important guests had left—all in a really good mood. The food, the company, everything had been highly appreciated.

'See, dear, you were uselessly throwing tantrums,' Ma said. 'Vanya is a really sweet child. Don't pretend now—I can make out you two had lots of fun together.'

'She's okay,' Samira pretended to yawn. Eeeks—a green spot still lingered on her wrist. Quickly she covered it with her hand. 'Yeah, I managed to tolerate her.'

Ma shook her head and smiled.

Samira smiled to herself too as she turned away thinking ... who'd have dreamt the time would come when she could share a joke with Vanya ... wouldn't dread her visits any more? Would even think of her as a friend? But she was not going to let Ma know that—as yet!

ACKNOWLEDGEMENTS

'A Caterpillar Called Matthew' was first published in *Children's World* Magazine brought out by Children's Book Trust, New Delhi; 'The Best Hanuman' first appeared in the anthology *Celebrate: Dussehra and Durga Puja*, published by Hachette India; 'My Life in Pictures' first appeared in the anthology *Mom and Me* published by Hachette India; 'Just Balloons' appeared in the *Readers' Club Bulletin* of the National Book Trust; 'Fire' and 'The Tough Decision' were first published in *Target* magazine, 'The Girl in the Garden' has appeared in my collection *The Mailbox Ghost and Other Spooky Stories* (Kindle ebook) 'Greenchickenpoxitis' was first published in the children's page of *The Pioneer*.

Other Books By the Same Author

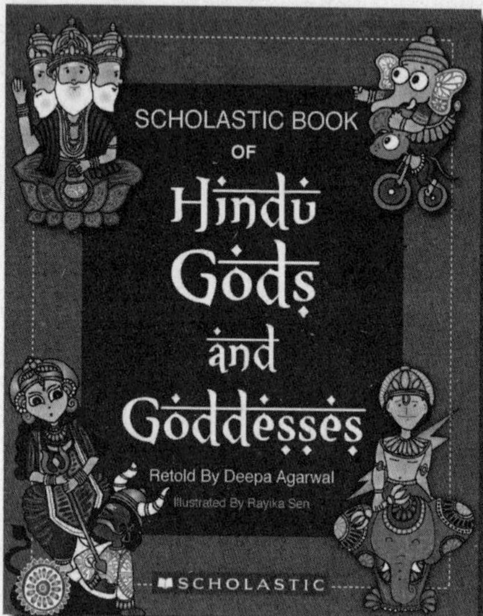